DRAGLINS

For Chris and Chris, with lots of love
xx VF

For Ancel Morgan, mentor!
Thank you.
CF

ORCHARD BOOKS
338 Euston Road, London NW1 3BH
Orchard Books Australia
Level 17/207, Kent Street, Sydney, NSW 2000
First published in Great Britain in 2007
First paperback publication 2008
Text © copyright Vivian French 2007
Illustrations © copyright Chris Fisher 2007
The rights of Vivian French and Chris Fisher to be
identified as the author and illustrator of this work
have been asserted by them in accordance with
the Copyright, Designs and Patents Act, 1988.

A CIP catalogue record for this book is
available from the British Library.

ISBN 978 1 84362 696 1 (hardback)
ISBN 978 1 84362 705 0 (paperback)

1 3 5 7 9 10 8 6 4 2 (hardback)
3 5 7 9 10 8 6 4 2 (paperback)
Printed in Great Britain
Orchard Books is a division of Hachette Children's Books,
an Hachette Livre UK company.
www.orchardbooks.co.uk

DRAGLINS ESCAPE!

VIVIAN FRENCH CHRIS FISHER

ORCHARD BOOKS

CHAPTER ONE

Scritch! Scratch! Scrabble scrabble...

"Dennis!" the voice was small and squeaky. "Dennis! Come back! We're not meant to be here – Aunt Plum'll kill us if she ever finds out!"

"I'm a dust monster!" said another voice, just as squeaky. "Wheee! Watch me fly!"

There was a second's silence, a sudden thump, then, "OUCH!"

"Serves you right," said the first voice smugly. "I told you not to...oh NO! Uncle Damson's coming this way! Quick! RUN!"

Pitter patter pitter patter patter...

The very old lady who lived in the top flat shook her head. She'd miss the little creatures who lived above her ceiling, although she'd never found out exactly what they were. They were no trouble – not like rats or mice.

Sometimes a biscuit or a slice of bread disappeared, but mostly they swept up her crumbs and took away her potato peelings. And any leftover sultanas. They loved sultanas.

The old lady sighed as she looked round at her boxes and bundles.

She was moving out today, and going to live with her niece in a smart modern house where not even the smallest of spiders was allowed. She loved her niece, but this had been her home for a long time.

RRRRRRRRRING! That was the doorbell. The very old lady picked up her suitcase...and paused.

"Silly old woman," she said to herself. "Silly old woman...but no one will ever know."

She looked up at the ceiling.

"Little creatures!" she called as loudly as she could in her wavery voice. "Little creatures! I'm going away, so do be careful! My dear old home is going to get a brand new roof! Goodbye now! Goodbye!"

And the very old lady smiled as she went out of the door.

Up above the ceiling, in the dark dusty roof space, there was a stunned silence.

CHAPTER TWO

The four little draglins sat in a row on the rusty gas pipe that ran across the length of the loft. They were waiting for Uncle Damson to speak. Aunt Plum had told them at breakfast time that he had Something Very Important to say to them when he came home from Collecting, and they had spent the day discussing what it might be.

Daffodil, who was optimistic whatever the circumstances, was wildly excited. She was certain that Uncle Damson was finally going to allow them to have a baby beetle as a pet. She'd been asking for a beetle for as long as she could remember, and although Aunt Plum had told her over and over again that a dusty roof space at the very top of a tall old house was no place for a pet, she remained ever hopeful.

Dora, who was always nervous and expecting the worst, thought Uncle Damson was going to say that he and Aunt Plum were getting too old to go out to work, and that they were all going to slowly starve to death. She was the only one of the little draglins who ever thought about the dangers her uncle and aunt faced when they were collecting food and other necessities for their family, and she expected tragedy daily.

Whenever Uncle Damson was late returning home Dora convinced herself that he had been attacked by a brid, or stung by a swap, or carried away by a fiercesome wirrel. It was all too easy for her to imagine her aunt and uncle sitting in their armchairs, wrinkled, toothless, and unable to move a step to feed their ever hungry nephews and nieces…

Dora blew her nose hard as she thought how sad it would be when all of them were a little row of bones. "And think of cousin Pip!" she said to Daffodil. "He's only a baby! His bones will be TINY!" And she blew her nose even harder.

"Rubbish," Daffodil said. "Don't be such an old worryguts!"

Danny was nervous too, but that was because he was feeling guilty. Normally feeling guilty was not something that Danny bothered about much, but the one rule that Uncle Damson insisted was never broken on pain of terrible punishment was NO SMOKING, and Danny and Dennis knew they'd had a smoke-blowing competition the day before.

On his better days Danny could understand that a dry wooden-beamed loft, full of piles of old newspaper and rubbish and dust, was a dreadful fire hazard, but Dennis always behaved as if

rules were made to be broken.

"It isn't as if we're going to breathe out *flames*," he told Danny. "It's only *smoke!*" Danny had allowed himself to be persuaded, and they had crept away from the neat area surrounded by piles of newspapers that was home to see if they could blow smoke rings. Somehow the smell of smoke had hung about them when they came back for tea, and still lingered in their sleeping space late that evening despite wild flappings of Danny's jumper. Aunt Plum hadn't said anything about it, but she had looked very thoughtful as she came in to say goodnight.

Dennis was sure Aunt Plum hadn't noticed anything. He said he thought Uncle Damson was going to tell them to be good tidy little draglins, because that was what he always said. And as none of them ever took any notice it wasn't worth worrying about...but if Uncle Damson DID say something different, then at least it'd be a change. Dennis said it was time something changed.

"I'm so BORED," he complained, and Danny and Daffodil groaned loudly. Dennis was always moaning about being bored. They were bored too, but they didn't go on and on and ON about it like Dennis.

"Every day's the same," Dennis went on. "Get up, have lessons, learn about chats and dawgs and how WE MUST BE VERY CAREFUL BECAUSE THEY ARE SO DANGEROUS. But it's just stupid telling us stuff like that. We never ever get out of here, so the worst thing we've ever had happen was when that eeb flew in. I want to have adventures! I want to SEE a chat! I tell you, if something doesn't change soon I'm going to go MAD!"

"Sh!" Dora said anxiously. "Don't say things like that! Change is scary!"

Dennis snorted. "Living in a dusty old place like this isn't MY idea of fun!" he said. "Nothing exciting EVER happens here!"

CHAPTER THREE

U ncle Damson cleared his throat. "Ahem!" he said. "Now, listen carefully!"

Daffodil wriggled forward to the edge of the gas pipe. Dennis nudged her, and she fell off with a loud squeak. Uncle Damson frowned as she giggled and picked herself up.

"This is very serious, Daffodil," he said in his fiercest voice. "PLEASE pay attention!"

Daffodil climbed back and did her best to look as if she was listening hard.

Uncle Damson coughed again. "Ahem," he said.

"We draglins have lived here ever since you four were hatched. We've been warm and safe and happy, and the Collecting has been easy. But now something very terrible has happened. Human Beanies are interfering in our lives, and our home is no longer safe. We have to move."

"MOVE?"

All four little draglins started talking at once. Dora was horrified. Danny wasn't sure what he was feeling. Both Daffodil and Dennis were as thrilled as if Uncle Damson had told them they could have an extra birthday.

"WHEN?" asked Danny. "When will we move? And where to?"

"Will it be to the Outdoors?" Daffodil said hopefully. "Where the sun shines?"

"I want to move NOW!" said Dennis.

"I don't want to move at all," Dora wailed.

Uncle Damson tapped his foot on the floorboards. "HUSH!" he said. "We'll be moving as soon as Aunt Plum and I have found somewhere suitable. And yes, Daffodil, it will most likely be in the Outdoors.

"We know all about Outdoors," Daffodil boasted. "Aunt Plum's told us!"

Dennis chipped in. "She's drawn us LOADS of pictures of chats chasing dawgs and brids chasing chats!"

"Oh, Dennis! That's the wrong way round!" Dora loved lessons.

"Whatever," said Dennis, who didn't. "We'll be just FINE, Uncle Damson!"

Uncle Damson folded his arms. "We'll see about that, young Dennis. It's a truly frightening and dangerous world once you leave Under Roof. That's why Aunt Plum and I have kept you safely here ever since you hatched...because we don't want you suffering – ahem! – the way I did."

Uncle Damson stopped, and glanced across at Aunt Plum. She nodded her head in a meaningful way.

"Ah. Yes." Uncle Damson was behaving so oddly the little draglins gazed at him in wonder. "Aunt Plum and I think that now is the time for me to show you something you may have noticed before, but never properly understood." He turned slowly round, and lowered his trousers just enough so Dennis, Daffodil, Danny and Dora could see the stump where his tail should have been.

"That, children," he said in a grand and solemn voice, "is what happens when a young and foolish draglin meets a chat."

It was lucky for Daffodil that Dora let out a loud wail. If Uncle Damson had heard her giggle he might have decided to risk staying Under Roof forever in order to keep her safe.

CHAPTER FOUR

The next day seemed very long. Uncle Damson and Aunt Plum disappeared early in the morning, and Dora and Danny were left to look after Pip. Daffodil and Dennis had instructions to help, but not to get him overexcited. Daffodil had taken this as a challenge, and had spent the day building Pip dust castles, and letting him roll in them. Dora had tried to clean him up but had made things worse, and he was covered in dirty smears and sneezing furiously.

"I'm very sorry," Dora said as Uncle Damson and Aunt Plum finally came back home. "I tried to wash him but he didn't like it."

"H'mph!" said Uncle Damson. "What that baby needs is a proper bath! And I need to rest my feet." He disappeared behind the cold water tank where he had a small space of his own that he called his study.

The little draglins weren't allowed to bother him there, so they were constantly peeping round the pipes...but Uncle Damson never seemed to do much more than sleep.

Aunt Plum sat down and sighed. "Maybe it's a good thing we're moving. The dust's been getting worse and worse recently. It'll be wonderful to be out in the fresh air—"

"Fresh air?" Daffodil pounced. "So we ARE going to live in the Outdoors!"

Dora shuddered. "Are we really, Aunt Plum?" she asked. "Have you found somewhere?"

Aunt Plum sighed again. "Yes," she said. "Well, we've found somewhere for the time being. We're going to move in with Plant and Puddle, and see how it works out."

Four pairs of wide eyes stared at Aunt Plum.

"PLANT AND PUDDLE?" said Daffodil. "Whoever are they?"

Aunt Plum looked at the little draglins, and smiled. "My brothers," she said.

"BROTHERS?" Dennis's eyes were popping. "You've got BROTHERS?"

"Oh yes," said Aunt Plum. "Plant and Puddle are your uncles. And there are aunts out there, too – and cousins."

For once even Daffodil and Dennis were silent. It was Danny who finally asked, "Why didn't we know about them? Do they know about us? Why didn't you tell us?"

"Uncle Damson didn't think you ought to know," Aunt Plum said slowly. "He thought it might make you unhappy. You see, we promised your parents we'd look after you if anything ever happened to them. And something did. The very worst thing ever. And Uncle Damson is very very careful to keep his promises, so he thought it would be best if you didn't know about the Outers – the outdoor draglins – in case you wanted to go out and find them...but then we heard that we had to leave. And yes, they do know about us."

Dennis and Daffodil and Danny and Dora looked at each other.

"WOW!" breathed Dennis. "That's BRILLIANT!"

Daffodil nodded enthusiastically. Danny grinned. Dora looked worried.

"I do hope so," Aunt Plum said. She got up slowly from her seat. "Erm...you may find that some of the Outers think we're a little strange. They don't like Human Beanie houses. Or being anywhere close to where Beanies are active. Not at all."

Dora said in a wobbly voice, "Do you mean they won't like us?"

"We'll be OK," Daffodil said cheerfully. "Just you wait and see!"

"They'll be our relations," Danny said, "so they can't be too bad. Can they?"

Aunt Plum suddenly became very brisk and busy. "Time for you all to get cleaned up before bed," she said. "Tell you what, why don't you all have a swim in the water tank? It may be the last time, after all!

We're going to move in the morning."

There was a loud cheer, even from Dora. Swimming in the water tank was a special treat, and not one they were often allowed in case the water got dirty, and the Beanies in the flats below noticed when they turned on their taps. They scrambled happily up the rafters, and Aunt Plum carried Pip up as well to give him a good scrub.

Even if the Beanies did notice dust in the water it wouldn't matter now. The draglins would be far away by the time they came to investigate.

CHAPTER FIVE

Dora, who had been awake and worrying all night long, lay on her sleeping mat and stared up into the shadowy rafters above her. The steep slated roof and rough splintery wood was the only sky she had ever known, and she couldn't quite believe it was going to change. She had never wanted anything to be different; she loved the cosy sameness of every day, and the thought of a huge strange outside world made her heart pit-a-pat with agitation.

"Come on, Dor!" Daffodil appeared beside her. "Get up! It's the best day of our lives! Aunt Plum says we've got to wrap our clothes and anything else we can't do without in our sleeping mats, and tie it all up. She says anything we don't really need has got to be left behind – we're going to have a brand new life in a brand new home!"

Dora looked round her. She'd have to take her collection of pigeon feathers, carefully arranged in order of size. And two small stones she'd found in a dusty corner. And a piece of bright red wool that Aunt Plum had Collected and was going to make into a jumper for Pip, but had never got round to using. Then there were her clothes, neatly folded in the space under the hot pipe by the water tank to keep warm.

Daffodil's things were thrown all over the sleeping space, as usual, and Daffodil was darting about in the middle of them, tossing a few onto her mat, but most into a corner.

"Daffodil!" Dora said indignantly as a yellow scarf flew past her ear. "That's MINE!"

"Ooops," Daffodil said. "Never mind. We'll have lots of new things when we move.

I'm going to ask Aunt Plum to make me LOADS of new dresses so the Outers can see we're REALLY important draglins and they'll want to be friends with us at once!"

Dora trotted off to fetch the scarf. It was made from a piece of a soft old duster, and she was fond of it.

"But where will Uncle Damson Collect things from?" she asked. "Aunt Plum said the new home wasn't near any Beanies." Her eyes filled with tears. "Oh, Daffodil – why can't we just stay here? I'm sure it would be all right..."

Daffodil snorted loudly and tied up the corners of her sleeping mat. It looked suspiciously empty. "If we stay here," she said, "we'll get Discovered. I heard Aunt and Uncle talking late last night.

The Beanies are going to pull the roof right off, so they'd be sure to see us! DO get on with it, Dora – look, I'll help you." And Daffodil grabbed a handful of Dora's feathers and tossed them in the air.

"No – I'll do it!" Dora wiped her eyes. "Just leave me alone, Daffy."

Daffodil snorted again, snatched up Dora's yellow scarf and wrapped it round her waist with a flourish. Then she went off to annoy Dennis and Danny.

CHAPTER SIX

hen Aunt Plum had finally got all four little draglins organised, together with their sleeping mat bundles, Uncle Damson appeared from behind the water tank. He was puffing a good deal, and pushing a huge bag in front of him. The very old lady from the flat downstairs would have recognised it as a plastic wash bag that had mysteriously disappeared from her bathroom. Uncle Plum opened the top of the bag with a flourish.

"Now," he instructed, "put your things in here. Aunt Plum and I have packed what we need, and now it's your turn. Dennis, you first!"

Dennis stepped forward, and dropped in his bundle. Danny and Daffodil followed, and finally Dora.

"Good!" Uncle Plum gave them a thumbs-up. "Now, help me to pull the string TIGHT!"

They grabbed hold of the string, and pulled and pulled until the bag was tightly shut. Uncle Damson climbed on top, and gave his orders.

"Danny, right over left. Daffodil, left over right – NO! RIGHT! Danny, you do it – that's better!" And the string was safely knotted.

"How can we ever get that great big bag all the way to Outdoors?" Dora whispered to Aunt Plum. "It's bigger than we are!"

"Sh, dear," Aunt Plum said. "Uncle Damson has a PLAN."

"Indeed I do," Uncle Damson said proudly. He slid off the wash bag, and marched over to where the roof slates reached the bottom rafter. With a flourish he pulled at a sliver of wood, and it broke away with a sharp snap. There was a grating noise as a slate slid down, hesitated, and slithered away, leaving a wide clear opening. It was followed by two more slates in quick succession. Early morning sunshine poured in, and for a moment everyone was dazzled. Far away down below there was a series of splintering crashes.

"WOW!" said Dennis. "GOOD one, Uncle Damson!"

Uncle Damson tried to hide his smile.

"Everyone ready to push?" he said. "The bag goes next!"

"Eeeeeeeeeeeek!" Dora's high-pitched shriek made everyone jump, and Pip began to cry.

"I CAN'T jump out of there!" she wailed. "I can't, I can't – I'd rather stay here and be bones forever than jump – PLEASE don't make me – PLEASE!"

"Silly child," Uncle Damson said crossly. "No one's asking you to jump anywhere. Go and stand over there and hold Pip's hand, and the boys and Daffodil can help me. It's only the bag that's going through the hole – we'll be going the way Aunt Plum and I always go."

Dora trailed off, and Uncle Damson organised Aunt Plum, Dennis, Danny and Daffodil into a row behind the large bulk of the wash bag. "When I say push, PUSH!" he said.

CHAPTER SEVEN

Dennis and Danny and Daffodil enjoyed the pushing and heaving at first. They became less enthusiastic when the bag got stuck on a splinter, and it took an age to work it free. Then Daffodil suddenly asked why they hadn't packed the bag right in front of the slates so it would only have taken one big push, and the air around Uncle Damson became extremely icy.

"Just stop talking and PUSH," he snapped. "All I'm asking for is a little co-operation here, Daffodil – not clever remarks."

Daffodil opened her mouth to say something else, but Danny trod hard on her foot and she squeaked instead. Uncle Damson took this as an apology, and began counting again.

"One, two, three, PUSH! One, two, three, PUSH!"

The bag inched nearer to the open space between the slates.

"Nearly there," Aunt Plum encouraged. "I think it'll only take one more push – so do be very careful, children. Daffodil – I think you'd better come behind me."

"I can push just as hard as everyone else," Daffodil said, not moving. "Just because I'm a girl doesn't mean I'm no use!"

"HUH!" Dennis made a face at her. "That's what YOU think!"

"Be quiet, Dennis," Uncle Damson said firmly. "Daffodil, you can stay where you are as long as you're sensible. Now, let's have one last push. Are you ready? One...two...three...PUSH!"

Uncle Damson, Aunt Plum, Dennis, Danny and Daffodil put their shoulders against the wash bag and gave a final heave. The bag teetered, wobbled, snagged against a slate and hung half in, half out of the roof.

"Oh NO!" said Danny.

"I expect we can loosen it," said Aunt Plum.

"I think it's coming away by itself," said Uncle Damson.

"WHEEEEEEE!" yelled Daffodil as she charged at the bag with her arms wide open.

The bag ripped free and plummeted downwards, only to stop with a jerk as the string caught on a bent nail. It swung wildly to and fro, but was completely anchored.

Daffodil had vanished.

CHAPTER EIGHT

There was a ghastly silence in Under Roof.

Then Dora said in a small clear voice, "Daffodil's DEAD, isn't she?" and burst into floods of tears.

Uncle Damson stood frozen to the spot.

Danny swallowed hard.

"WAAAAH!" yelled Pip.

Aunt Plum, looking pale, hurried across to hug Dora and Pip both at the same time.

"Now now," she said, "we don't know anything yet. Draglins have been known to fall from enormous heights quite safely."

"Yeah," said Dennis. "And we're talking Daffodil here!" He swung himself out on the bent nail and peered down at the garden below.

"Can't see anything," he reported cheerfully.

"She's not splatted on the hard stony bit, and there's no sign of her on that green hairy stuff – what's that called again. Aunt Plum?"

"Griss," Aunt Plum said, automatically.

"Yes, griss." Dennis pulled himself back inside. "There's a lot of green leafy stuff bouncing about down there on stalks ("Boshes," Aunt Plum said quietly) but I can't see any sign of her."

Aunt Plum folded her arms. "There's only one thing to do," she said. "We'll have to leave now this minute, and look for Daffodil."

"Yes. Yes, of course." Uncle Damson pulled himself together with an effort. "Right. Everyone follow me. Plum, you'd best take up the rear with Pip. Now, no squeaking or whispering. Silence is the word, and we'll be out there to see...to see what's happened in the twinkle of an eye..." Uncle Damson stopped to cough. "Ahem! Time to go!"

Dennis, Danny and a sobbing Dora followed on tiptoe as Uncle Damson strode under the water tank into ever deepening shadow. Aunt Plum scurried behind holding Pip, every so often giving a little sniff.

Further and further into the darkness they went, until Uncle Damson stopped at what seemed to be a solid brick wall.

"Now," he said, "we must be very careful.

From now on we'll be going down through the places where Human Beanies live. Not a sound from any of you!" He pushed at a chipped and smoke-blackened half-brick, and to the little draglins' amazement it swung round. Behind it was a deep hole that dropped into complete darkness.

Dora put her hands over her mouth to smother her squeak, and Aunt Plum patted her shoulder. "It's not as bad as it looks," she whispered. "Feel for the rope! It goes all the way down."

"SSSH!" Uncle Plum hissed at them. "Hurry up! We don't know..." his voice began to shake again. "Ahem, ahem-ahem-ahem AHEM. Let's be as quick as we can!" And he climbed into the hole and disappeared. Dennis followed with a cheery wave at Under Roof, and Danny slid silently after him.

Dora took a deep breath, shut her eyes and hoped for the best. She was pleased to find that Aunt Plum was right, and a strong rope was there for her to hang on to...a rope Collected by Uncle Damson many years ago from the very old lady's string box. Even though Dora couldn't see anything she could hear Danny puffing just below her, and Aunt Plum soothing Pip as she c l i m b e d steadily down behind.

"I can do it!" she said to herself.

"I MUST do it...or I might never see Daffodil again!"

On and on and on they went. Dora became aware that from time to time horizontal tunnels led away from the tunnel they were swinging down, and several times she heard strange and unfamiliar sounds horribly close by. There were rustlings, and a noise like Uncle Damson snoring only a hundred times louder, and the whoosh of running water,

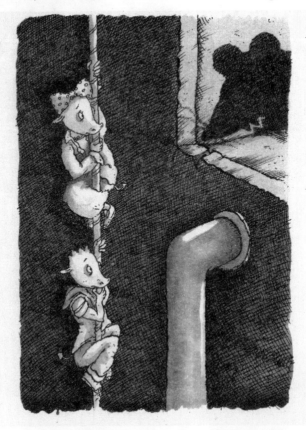

and then, all of a sudden, a sharp yapping noise that made Aunt Plum give a strange little gasp.

"Dawg," Aunt Plum muttered to herself. "Oh, POOR little Daffodil!"

A moment later fresh air was flooding up round them, and then dim light...and at long last they tumbled out of the end of the tunnel onto a rough stone floor.

CHAPTER TEN

Dennis, Danny and Dora stared. And stared. And stared.

"This," Uncle Damson told them as he picked himself up, "is what Human Beanies call a basement. This is where the Metal Monster lives. The Beanies feed it coal and wood, and it roars fire and blows heat all the way to Under Roof."

Dora remembered the hot pipe that had kept her clothes warm, and shuddered. Uncle Damson had never said it was heated with monster breath.

Dennis was already scrambling over heaps of coal. "Which way's out, Uncle Damson?" he asked cheerily. "I want to see Outdoors!"

"Me too!" said Danny.

"I want to find poor Daffodil," Dora said, and hiccupped loudly.

Uncle Damson frowned. "Ssssh! We must be VERY quiet! ANYTHING might be outside waiting for us..." and he began to creep towards a heavy wooden door. Sunlight beamed a bright yellow haze underneath, and even Dora felt a little more cheerful as she tiptoed after Danny.

Uncle Damson reached the door, and bent down to peer first one way and then the other through the gap underneath.

"Nothing there," he reported.

"Oh oh oh OH!" Dora wailed.

"SSSHHH!" Uncle Damson was cross. "How many times must I tell you, Dora?

There might be a chat out there, or a dawg, or even a Beanie watching...although Beanies are usually asleep at this time of day. Now, the Underground is only a few steps across the stones. It's safe in there. I want you all to run across just as fast as you can go, and wait for me there."

"Why?" asked Dennis. "What are you going to do?"

At the same moment Danny asked, "What's the Underground?"

"I'm going to look for Daffodil, of course," Uncle Damson snapped angrily. "And the Underground's a safe passage to the other end of the garden. You'll find out all about it when we get there. Now, STOP ASKING QUESTIONS!"

An odd look came over Dennis's face. Dora saw it, and moaned faintly. Dennis was Going To Be Difficult.

"*I* want to look for Daffodil," Dennis growled. "Me and Danny should be the ones to look. She's OUR sister!"

Dora waited for the storm to break. Surprisingly, it didn't. Uncle Damson said in quite a mild tone, "Fair enough. We'll ALL look. But let me check first, there's a good lad."

Dennis hesitated, and then nodded, and Uncle Damson vanished into the sunlight.

It seemed an age to the waiting draglins before he came back. Dennis began to look mutinous.

"He'll be checking the entrance to the Underground," Aunt Plum explained soothingly. "Outside this door there's a Human Beanie path, and beyond that there's a grissy slope. The Underground's in the thick of the griss, but sometimes leaves fall off the boshes on the top, and the entrance gets blocked and needs clearing out. Uncle Damson'll want to make sure we can run straight in."

"I think we should go *now*." Dennis looked at Danny. "What do you think, Danny?"

Danny didn't even have time to open his mouth before Uncle Damson came bustling back.

"Right!" he said. "The Underground's clear. Dennis – you look up and down the path – but DON'T go anywhere else! Danny, you go with him, and make sure neither of you does anything foolish. When you get to the boundary walls, come straight back. I'll look under the boshes, and Plum – you and Dora and Pip search in the griss. And if I whistle, you're all to RUN to the round brick hole you'll see opposite – that's the Underground. Beanies think it's a drain. Straight in there, and no messing! Even the chats can't catch us in there."

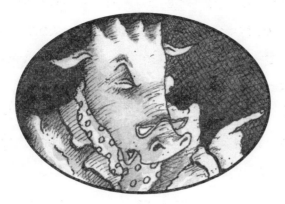

CHAPTER ELEVEN

The sunshine was dazzling. Dennis, Danny and Dora, used to living in the dim half-light of Under Roof, blinked and squinted as they crept out from under the basement door of the huge old tenement flats. Pip began to coo and burble, and Aunt Plum rubbed her eyes.

"Wow!" Dora breathed, "it's — it's beautiful!" Her lip began to tremble. "I do wish Daffodil was here..."

"Cheer up, stupid!" Dennis said in his most encouraging voice. "We're just about to find her! Come on, Danny — let's get looking!" And he shot away down the path in a series of zigzags. Danny followed slowly. Uncle Damson looked after them with a worried expression on his face.

"H'm," he said. "I hope they don't get into any trouble..."

"You had a good look round when you came out here just now, didn't you?" Aunt Plum asked.

"Of course I did." Uncle Damson sounded indignant. "Do you think I'd let those two boys run around without making sure it was safe first?"

"Well then. We'll just have to hope for the best," Aunt Plum said. "Come along Dora. We'll go and hunt in the—"

"YAP! YAP YAP YAP YAP! YAP YAP!"

Aunt Plum froze. The noise wasn't coming from the flats, but from somewhere in the garden above them.

"Dawg!" Uncle Damson whispered. "Dawg – and it's after something!"

Dora clutched at Aunt Plum's hand.

"HEY!" Dennis suddenly appeared beside Aunt Plum. His eyes were shining with excitement. "There's a DAWG!" he gasped. "And it's shouting its head off! Danny's climbing up a house pole ("pain dripe," Aunt Plum muttered) to see if he can see where it is and what it's doing!"

Uncle Damson's mouth opened and shut several times before he managed to splutter, "Danny's doing WHAT?"

"Climbing a house pole! Hey, Uncle Damson! If we go up to the top of the slope we can see for ourselves!" And Dennis was just about to shoot off when Uncle Damson caught him by his jacket.

"NO!" he hissed urgently, "NO! You'll get eaten!"

"NAH! Not me! But Daffodil might be!" Dennis gave a quick, violent wriggle, and poor Uncle Damson was left holding an empty sleeve as Dennis shot across the path.

Dora squeaked, "DAFFODIL!" and rushed after him.

"DORA!" roared Uncle Damson, "DENNIS! DANNY! Come BACK!"

There was no answer.

Uncle Damson groaned, and sank down in a heap in the middle of the path.

Aunt Plum shook her head, then marched briskly across to the Underground entrance.

She plonked Pip inside, and pulled a sultana out of her bag.

"Good boy," she said. "Now, stay right here. Mama will be back in two ticks!"

"Gooo!" said Pip, grabbing the sultana. "Gooo! Sultana!"

Aunt Plum smiled fondly at him, then strode back to Uncle Damson and heaved him to his feet.

"Damson," she said, "it's time for action!" And she and Uncle Damson hurried after Dora in between the thick green grass stalks.

CHAPTER TWELVE

Danny had always been the best at climbing, and the drain pipe was as easy as a roof beam. He whizzed up until he was well above the top of the slope, and could see over the bushes and shrubs that crowded together beyond it. In among the bushes was a gap where a small tree was doing its best to grow, and Danny's eyes grew wide as he saw a black and white terrier dancing round and round the twisted trunk. It was yapping and snapping and snarling, and making angry little leaps in the air.

Up in the branches a bright yellow scarf was waving valiantly.

"DAFFODIL! Oi!" yelled Danny. "DAFFODIL!" but the dog was making far too much noise for him to be heard.

Danny looked to left and right to make sure he would know where the tree was when he was on ground level, and then skittered down the drain pipe as fast as he could go.

"Uncle Damson!" he panted as he reached the path, "Uncle Damson! I've found her!"

But there was no Uncle Damson or Aunt Plum to be seen. Only Pip waving from the entrance to the Underground.

"Oh, THUNDER!" Danny hurled himself at the slope and began scrambling up. On and on he went until he found himself grabbing at the roots of a lavender bush, and the yapping was deafeningly loud. With a wriggle Danny was past the lavender – and found himself face to face with a very surprised Dora.

"I've found her!" Danny whispered breathlessly. "She's hanging on to the top of a little tree!"

Dora was so thrilled she flung her arms round Danny and cheered loudly. "Hurrah!" she shrieked in her shrill little voice. "HURRAH!"

The yapping stopped.

There was a sudden frozen silence, and then a sniffing...

And a snuffling...

And it was getting nearer...

Danny unhooked himself from Dora's hug, but held on to her arm. "QUICK!" he said. "It HEARD you! Back down to the Underground – and keep cheering! Make it follow us! Come on! RUN! And keep cheering – One two three HURRAH!"

And the two little draglins plunged back down the slope as the black and white terrier came charging after them.

"YAP YAP!" it barked, "YAP!"

"Come on, dawg!" Danny yelled, and Dora squeaked, "HURRAH! HURRAH! HURRAH!" until her throat was sore and she was completely out of breath...and the Underground entrance was right in front of them. They tumbled inside with a whoop of triumph.

"Goooo," said Pip, and Dora began to sob with relief and delayed terror.

CHAPTER THIRTEEN

It was a good five minutes before the terrier stopped sniffing round the Underground entrance. Danny heard someone whistle over and over again, and at last the dog trotted away.

"Phew," said Danny. "Thank goodness! Shall we go and look for the others?"

"NO." Dora shook her head wildly. "They'll come back here, and if we aren't here they'll go looking for us, and then we'll have to look for them some more, and we'll never ever ever find each other again!"

"Very sensible of you, young Dora," said a voice, and Uncle Damson came into view in the entrance. He was holding Daffodil in a firm grip, but she was looking hugely pleased with herself. Aunt Plum and Dennis were close behind.

"Daffodil!" Dora hurled herself at her sister and hugged her tightly.

"Hi!" Daffodil said cheerfully. "Guess what? I flew out of the roof and I landed in a tree and I've been chased by a dawg and I made it run away and now I'm here – I LIKE being Outdoors!"

She sat down by Dora with a flump. "You'd have been EVER so scared, Dor."

Danny stood up. "Actually, Daffodil," he said, "it was Dora that saved you."

"It was ME that saved Daffodil!" Dennis was indignant. "I whistled and whistled and WHISTLED until the dawg ran away! AND it was me that saw it first!"

"And very nearly got snapped up for its dinner," Uncle Damson said sourly.

"No I didn't," Dennis argued, but Aunt Plum hushed him.

"The most important thing is that we're all together again," she said. "Now, follow Uncle Damson!"

And Uncle Damson led the way down the Underground. It was dim, but never completely dark, and it wound round and round. There were crossroads and side roads, but Uncle Damson never hesitated, and at last they saw daylight ahead.

"There!" he said, and there was pride in his voice. "There! There's our new home!" The four little draglins stared.

Beyond the Underground exit was a broken down wooden shed that had once belonged to Human Beanies. It was raised on bricks, and to a Beanie eye it would look as if there was nothing but sticks and rubbish under the floorboards. The four little draglins saw a neat little front door – a front door that was wide open. Standing in front of it were two draglins, one very fat, and the other very thin. They were looking towards the Underground.

From inside the house a faint wisp of smoke curled into the air.

"Who are they?" Dora whispered.

"Those," said Aunt Plum, "are your uncles. Uncle Plant and Uncle Puddle. By the smell of that smoke, they've been cooking a Welcome Stew. Come along, children. Welcome to your new home."

Dennis, Danny, Daffodil and Dora didn't move. They were suddenly stricken with shyness.

In all their lives they had never seen any grown-up draglins other than Aunt Plum and Uncle Damson, and now they were facing two unknown uncles...and an unknown world.

The very fat draglin waddled into the house. He came back carrying a shiny black beetle wearing a bright red collar.

"Which is Daffodil?" he asked in a deep and growly voice.

Daffodil's eyes lit up. "ME!" she said breathlessly. "ME!"

"Heard you wanted a pet," Uncle Plant growled. "So here you are."

"It's BEAUTIFUL!" Daffodil gasped. She ran forward, and hugged Uncle Plant and the beetle together. "THANK YOU!"

"Ha," said Uncle Plant. "Ha. Glad you like it." He peered at Dora. "Want one too?"

Dora went very pink. "Erm…no thank you," she said. "I mean…"

Uncle Puddle nodded at her in a comforting way. "Prickly things, beetles," he said. "We'll find you something prettier. And—" he winked at Danny and Dennis. "Guess you two might like a mowser? Learnt to ride, yet?"

Danny's mouth dropped wide open.

"RIDE?" Dennis couldn't believe his ears. "Ride a MOWSER? US? WOW and ZIPPIDEE DOO DA!"

Aunt Plum made a loud tutting noise. "No need to spoil them the second they arrive, Puddle!" she said briskly. "Now, come along, everyone. We don't want that Welcome Stew to be ruined!"

And she swept Pip and Uncle Damson towards the front door. The two uncles followed, and for a moment Danny, Daffodil, Dora and Dennis were alone.

"This is GOOD," Dennis said, and his face was one big smile.

"VERY good," said Danny.

"Just MARVELLOUS!" Daffodil agreed, and she patted her beetle.

Dora looked round, and shivered. "It's so BIG," she said. "But..."

"Yes?" Daffodil prompted her.

"It'll be all right," Dora said slowly.

"Children! Hurry up and wash your hands!" It was Aunt Plum.

"COMING!" called the little draglins, and they hurried inside.

by Vivian French
illustrated by Chris Fisher

All priced at £3.99.

Draglins books are available from all good bookshops,
or can be ordered direct from the publisher:
Orchard Books, PO BOX 29, Douglas IM99 1BQ.
Credit card orders please telephone 01624 836000
or fax 01624 837033 or visit our website:
www.orchardbooks.co.uk
or e-mail: bookshop@enterprise.net for details.

To order please quote title, author and ISBN
and your full name and address.
Cheques and postal orders should be made
payable to 'Bookpost plc.'

Postage and packing is FREE within the UK
(overseas customers should add £2.00 per book).

Prices and availability are subject to change.